RADIO WORKS

1946–48

ANTONIN ARTAUD

RADIO WORKS

1946–48

TRANSLATED BY
CLAYTON ESHLEMAN

EDITED AND WITH AN AFTERWORD BY
STEPHEN BARBER

INTRODUCTION BY
ROS MURRAY

DIAPHANES

Ros Murray

Introduction

To have done with the judgement of god is the culmination of Artaud's project to create a new body, one which
would do away with the tired old corporeal forms that
he had spent most of his life hammering into dust; sometimes even quite literally as he struck his work and his
own body. It is here that Artaud's 'body without organs'
emerges for the first time, dancing 'inside out', as he
writes: 'that inside out will be his true side out' (p. 55).
When Artaud learned that the program he had recorded
would be censored, and would not be broadcast, he wrote,
in a letter to publisher Jean Paulhan, that 'it's a DISASTER
for me' (p. 88). Reduced to words on a page, stripped of
their frenzied, chanting, corporeal resonance, the texts
that Artaud wrote for the recording, reproduced here, lose
something of their magic. It is a recording designed to be
heard, not read, and readers are advised when approach-
ing this work to listen to the recordings, now easily accessible online.[1] Nonetheless, these are powerful words, and
as with all of Artaud's writing, especially towards the
end of his life after his release from the Rodez asylum,
which was arguably his most intensely creative period,
it is impossible to read these words without being struck
by their performative dimension. One is never simply a
reader of Artaud, as Artaud never simply wrote; his work
is full of noise and interference, borne out through wild
gesture, screams, glossolalic outbursts and a-signifying

marks on the page. His work is meant to be felt, not rationally comprehended, and it invariably draws attention to its own material status. Boring holes in his pages, he highlights the fragility and resistance of paper, and proposes not simply doing away with representation, but attacking the means through which representation and signification are expressed. The performance, understood as an enacting of magical forces, does away with the spectacle.

Roland Barthes calls Artaud's writing a 'writing out loud' ('écriture à haute voix'),[2] a description that seems all the more apt in relation to the radio texts. But this seems to apply just as readily to his notebooks, which are covered in noise: capital letters evoking the shouting that accompanied their coming into being, depictions of noisy, torturous machines, pages filled to the brim with frenzied pencil marks, in addition to interference from the grain of the paper itself. Artaud feeds off the interplay of different media, inventing new forms in the spaces between these. Bodily fluids and substances abound, and Artaud continually emphasises these both through his words and physically on his pages, leaving all kinds of stains and residue. He writes about sperm, sweat, flesh, blood, bone, shit, meat, breath, gas and farts. All of these are used to fight the battle against the organs, against representation, against religion, governments, ideas, philosophy and established order.

Whilst Artaud battles against the organisation of the body, it is striking how ordered this disordering is; how, through the chaos of bodily revolt, Artaud distils and organises ('to a hair / in a fulminating order', p. 15) his texts and ritualistic, glossolalic chants, choosing his words with precision. For these are not simply psychotic outbursts. *Pour en finir avec le jugement de dieu* is shot through with conscious performance of madness, in which Artaud pre-empts his critics in a staged dialogue, akin to an interview with a psychiatric doctor ('you are raving, Mr. Artaud', p. 51). In this disorderly ordering we catch glimpses of humour, one of Artaud's ultimate, yet often overlooked, forms of revolt ('is god a being? if he is it is made of shit. If he is not, he's not', p. 33), often enacted through the wild intonation (see the singsong recital of 'a little of his sperm' in the opening text), dramatic pauses, and gaps left on the page.

Artaud's work is performative in the sense that it never simply describes, but actively produces the events it enacts. As Austin characterises performative language, 'the issuing of the utterance is the performing of an action'.[3] Artaud's work, performed correctly, is magical, finding its power in ritualistic chanting. Intonation is key to this, recalling what he wrote about metaphysical language in *The Theatre and its Double*, where the aim is 'to deal with intonations in an absolutely concrete manner, restoring their power to shatter as well as really to manifest something; to turn against language and its basely utilitarian, one could say alimentary sources, against its trapped-beast origins; and finally, to consider language as a form of *incantation*'.[4] Given the emphasis Artaud places on performance, one cannot approach this work without also remembering that it was performed by, in addition to Artaud himself, three others: Roger Blin, Artaud's old friend and collaborator from the early 1930s, Paule Thévenin, a new friend who secured Artaud's legacy when she went on to edit his *Œuvres complètes*, and María Casarès, the Spanish actress who two years later became the unforgettable face of death in Jean Cocteau's *Orphée* (1950), a film in which Blin also appeared. Paule Thévenin's influence was significant – not only did she suggest Casarès when Artaud's friend Colette Thomas pulled out – but she also chose the text she wanted to read, giving the overall project a subtly shifted perspective, including one of Artaud's more counter-philosophical texts, and providing a sense of equilibrium with Casarès' recital of the text depicting the Tarahumara Tutuguri ritual.

Stripped of the interludes of Artaud's *bruitages*, screams, xylophone and kettle drum beating, the structure of the text on the page almost appears akin to that of the classical drama that Artaud so vehemently despised: it is in five parts, with the climax in Roger Blin's performance of the centrepiece (the most memorable moment for many of those who listen to the recording for the first time is Blin's sudden, unexpected cry, 'LE CACA'), with a prologue and conclusion both read by Artaud, the former setting the scene in the first part, the latter with the incredible denouement, introducing, for the first time, the spectacle-shattering body without organs (which Deleuze and Guattari borrowed as their anti-Capitalist, anti-Oedipal entity). Artaud had engaged classical form in his project *Les Cenci*, an early attempt at the enactment of the theatre of cruelty, but, as always, with the intention of disrupting and exploding verbal language, in favour instead of creating an affective, overwhelming experience. In this sense, *Pour en finir avec le jugement de dieu* could constitute a return to the theatre projects.

In *The Theatre and its Double* Artaud wrote that he wanted to treat his audience like snakes, perceiving physically through vibration, arguing that 'we can physically reduce the soul to a bundle of vibrations'[5] coming up with all kinds of methods through which this might be possible (through sound, music, lighting and revolving chairs). A radio broadcast allows for such forms of perception, where we can listen pressed right up against the speaker, like the Tarahumara who eat their peyote right out of ('à même') the earth. For it is when Artaud can no longer stand the suffocation, as he is 'pressed right up to my body' (p. 47), that the revolt is enacted: 'it is then that I shattered everything' (p. 47). As the post-scriptum, not read out in the recording, announces, from these fragments 'a new body will be assembled' (p. 79). Artaud manipulates the space of his body, and the space around his body, infusing all of his work with gesture, with ritual, and with incantation.

It is a work of rupture, with the rupturing of representation enacted through the rupture of surfaces, whether that is the skin (the 'itchings of intolerable eczema', p. 67) play out on the scratched and broken surface of the page itself), the suffocation-battling breath, the digestive tract, the vocal chords or the eardrums. Between the 'infinite outside' and the 'infinitesimal inside' (p. 33) there is always a surface to be destroyed. Even the word 'caca' enacts rupture, the repetition of the voiceless velar plosive /k/ requiring obstruction of the airflow, followed by the release of the 'a'. 'Caca' ('poo' in English) also refers to the Ancient Egyptian god Kha, the spirit-double that accompanies a human being throughout their life; in the post-scriptum of the text 'The Theatre of Cruelty' Artaud reminds us of the body dancing 'in blocks of / KHA, KHA' (p. 75).

A new space is thus created through this strange dance, diffused through vocal gesture across the airways, but the question arises: when does this revolt occur? The recording was not broadcast, and we are thrown back towards a very Artaudian form of temporality, in which the apocalypse, the all-engulfing destruction and recreation of the new body is suspended, continually put on hold. 'Not yet' is an expression repeated throughout these texts: 'the world is not yet formed' (p. 33), reality is 'not yet completed' (p. 63), the foetuses are 'still to be born' (p. 49) (like Artaud's self-constructed army of 'daughters of the heart to be born'), dance and theatre 'have not yet begun to exist' (p. 71). Artaud's verb tenses are also significant in this respect; the enactment of his project very often occurs in the future tense ('a new body / will be assembled', p. 79), or, less often, in the past, but rarely, as you might expect, in the present. But perhaps this is the ideal temporality for Artaud's magic counter-force, designed to revolt against his ECT-damaged, starved, drugged, cancer-ridden body. When Marshall McLuhan describes radio as 'a subliminal echo chamber of magical power to touch remote and forgotten chords';[6] it is hard to think of a more appropriate vehicle for Artaud's recordings. One can only imagine the impact this would have had, had it been broadcast on 2 February 1948, just over a month before Artaud's death: dancing over the airwaves, Artaud creates an inside-out counter-body, an inside-out counter-philosophy, an inside-out counter-theatre, and a full-scale sensory attack on all forms of representation.

NOTES

1 For example on Ubuweb: http://www.ubu.com/sound/artaud.html (last accessed 28 August 2020).

2 Roland Barthes, *Œuvres complètes*, vol. II (Paris: Seuil, 1995), p. 1528.

3 *Words* (Oxford: Clarendon, 1975), p. 6.

4 Artaud, *Œuvres complètes*, vol. IV (Paris: Gallimard, 1978), p. 45.

5 Artaud, *Œuvres complètes*, vol. IV (Paris: Gallimard, 1978), p. 127.

6 Marshall McLuhan, *Understanding Media* (London and New York: Routledge, 2001), p. 329.

POUR EN FINIR

AVEC LE JUGEMENT

DE DIEU

To have done with the judgement of God

kré
kré
pek
kre
e
pte

Il faut que tout
soit rangé
à un poil près
dans un ordre
fulminant.

puc te
puk te
li le
pek ti le
kruk

kré	Everything must	puc te
kré	be arranged	puk te
pek	to a hair	li le
kre	in a fulminating	pek ti le
e	order.	kruk
pte		

J'ai appris hier

(il faut croire que je retarde, ou peut-être n'est-ce
     qu'un faux bruit, l'un de ces sales ragots comme
     il s'en colporte entre évier et latrines à l'heure
     de la mise aux baquets des repas une fois de plus
     ingurgités),

j'ai appris hier

l'une des pratiques officielles les plus sensation-
     nelles des écoles publiques américaines

et qui font sans doute que ce pays se croit à la
     tête du progrès.

Il paraît que, parmi les examens ou épreuves que
     l'on fait subir à un enfant qui entre pour la pre-
     mière fois dans une école publique, aurait lieu
     l'épreuve dite de la liqueur séminale ou du sperme,

et qui consisterait à demander à cet enfant nouvel
     entrant un peu de son sperme afin de l'insérer
     dans un bocal

et de le tenir ainsi prêt à toutes les tentatives de
     fécondation artificielle qui pourraient ensuite
     avoir lieu.

Car de plus en plus les Américains trouvent qu'ils
     manquent de bras et d'enfants,

c'est-à-dire non pas d'ouvriers

mais de soldats,

et ils veulent à toute force et par tous les moyens
     possibles faire et fabriquer des soldats

en vue de toutes les guerres planétaires qui
     pourraient ultérieurement avoir lieu,

et qui seraient destinées à *démontrer* par les
     vertus écrasantes de la force

I learned yesterday
(you must think that I'm very slow, or perhaps it is
    only a false rumor, some of the dirty gossip that
    is peddled between the sink and the latrines at
    the hour when the buckets are filled with meals
    once again regurgitated),
I learned yesterday
about one of the most sensational official practices
    of the American public schools
which no doubt make that country consider itself at
    the head of progress.
Apparently, among the examinations or tests that a
    child has to undergo on entering a public school
    for the first time is the one called the
    seminal liquid or sperm test,
which consists of asking this newly-enrolled child
    for a little of his sperm in order to put it into a
    glass jar
and of thereby keeping it ready for all the attempts
    at artificial insemination which might
    eventually take place.
For more and more the Americans find that they
    lack manpower and children,
that is, not workers,
but soldiers,
and at all costs and by all possible means they want
    to make and manufacture soldiers
in view of all the planetary wars which might sub-
    sequently take place,
and which would be destined to *demonstrate* by the
    crushing virtues of force

la surexcellence des produits américains,
et des fruits de la sueur américaine sur tous les
    champs de l'activité et du dynamisme possible de
    la force.
Parce qu'il faut produire,
il faut par tous les moyens de l'activité possibles
    remplacer la nature partout où elle peut être
    remplacée,
il faut trouver à l'inertie humaine un champ majeur,
il faut que l'ouvrier ait de quoi s'employer,
il faut que des champs d'activités nouvelles soient créés,
où ce sera le règne enfin de tous les faux produits
    fabriqués,
de tous les ignobles ersatz synthétiques
où la belle nature vraie n'a que faire,
et doit céder une fois pour toutes et honteusement
    la place à tous les triomphaux produits de
    remplacement
où le sperme de toutes les usines de fécondation
    artificielle
fera merveille
pour produire des armées et des cuirassés.
Plus de fruits, plus d'arbres, plus de légumes,
    plus de plantes pharmaceutiques ou non et
    par conséquent plus d'aliments,
mais des produits de synthèse à satiété,
dans des vapeurs,
dans des humeurs spéciales de l'atmosphère, sur des
    axes particuliers des atmosphères tirées de force
    et par synthèse aux résistances d'une nature qui
    de la guerre n'a jamais connu que la peur.
Et vive la guerre, n'est-ce pas ?
Car n'est-ce pas, ce faisant, la guerre que les
    Américains ont préparée et qu'il prépare
    ainsi pied à pied.
Pour défendre cet usinage insensé contre toutes les
    concurrences qui ne sauraient manquer de
    toutes parts de s'élever,

the superexcellence of American products,
and the fruits of American sweat in all the fields
    of activity and potential dynamism of
    force.
Because there must be production,
nature must be replaced wherever it can be replaced
    by every possible means of
    activity,
a major field must be found for human inertia,
the worker must be kept busy at something,
new fields of activity must be created,
where all the false manufactured products,
all the ignoble synthetic ersatzes will finally reign,
where beautiful true nature has nothing to do,
and must give up its place once and for all and
    shamefully to all the triumphant replacement
    products,
where sperm from all the artificial insemination
    factories
will work miracles
to produce armies and battleships.
No more fruit, no more trees, no more
    vegetables, no more plants pharmaceutical
    or not and consequently no more food,
but synthetic products to repletion,
in vapors,
in special humors of the atmosphere, on particu-
    lar axes of atmospheres drawn by force and by
    synthesis from the resistance of a nature that has
    never known anything about war except fear.
And long live war, right?
For by doing this, it is war, isn't it, that the
    Americans have prepared for and that they
    prepare for thus step by step.
To defend this insane machining against all the
    competition which would inevitably break out
    on all sides,

il faut des soldats, des armées, des avions, des cuirassés,
de là ce sperme
auquel il paraîtrait que les gouvernements de
l'Amérique auraient eu le culot de penser.
Car nous avons plus d'un ennemi
et qui nous guette, mon fils,
nous, les capitalistes-nés,
et parmi ces ennemis
la Russie de Staline
qui ne manque pas non plus de bras armés.
Tout cela est très bien,
mais je ne savais pas les Américains un peuple si guerrier
Pour se battre il faut recevoir des coups
et j'ai vu peut-être beaucoup d'Américains à la guerre
mais ils avaient toujours devant eux d'incommensurables armées de tanks,
d'avions, de cuirassés
qui leur servaient de bouclier.
J'ai vu beaucoup se battre des machines
mais je n'ai vu qu'à l'infini
derrière
les hommes qui les conduisaient.
En face du peuple qui fait manger à ses chevaux,
à ses bœufs et à ses ânes les dernières tonnes de
morphine vraie qui peuvent lui rester pour la
remplacer par des ersatz de fumée,
j'aime mieux le peuple qui mange à même la terre
le délire d'où il est né,
je parle des Tarahumaras
mangeant le Peyotl à même le sol
pendant qu'il naît,
et qui tue le soleil pour installer le royaume de la
nuit noire,
et qui crève la croix afin que les espaces de l'espace ne
puissent plus jamais se rencontrer ni se croiser.

C'est ainsi que vous allez entendre la danse du
TUTUGURI.

there must be soldiers, armies, airplanes, battleships,
therefore this sperm
which the American governments have apparently
     had the nerve to consider.
For we have more than one enemy
and one who watches us, kid,
us, the born capitalists,
and among these enemies
Stalin's Russia
which is not short of armed men either.
All this is very fine,
but I did not know that the Americans were such a
     warlike people.
To fight you must receive blows
and perhaps I have seen many Americans at war
but in front of them they always had incommensu-
     rable armies of tanks, planes, battleships
serving as a shield.
I saw a lot of machines fight
but I saw only in the infinite
                    rear
the men who drove them.
Confronted by a people who make their horses,
     oxen and donkeys eat the last tons of true mor-
     phine which may be left to them in order to
     replace it with ersatz smoke,
I prefer the people who eat right out of the earth the
     delirium that gave birth to them,
I am speaking of the Tarahumaras
who eat Peyote straight from the soil
while it is born,
and who kill the sun in order to establish the king-
     dom of black night,
and who split the cross so that the spaces of space
     will never again meet or cross.

In this way you will hear the dance of the
     TUTUGURI.

Tutuguri

Le rite du soleil noir

Et en bas, comme au bas de la pente amère,
cruellement désespérée du cœur,
s'ouvre le cercle des six croix,
                très en bas,
comme encastré dans la terre mère,
désencastré de l'étreinte immonde de la mère
                qui bave.

La terre de charbon noir
est le seul emplacement humide
dans cette fente de rocher.

Le Rite est que le nouveau soleil passe par sept
        points avant d'éclater à l'orifice de la terre.

Et il y a six hommes,
un pour chaque soleil,
et un septième homme
qui est le soleil tout
                cru
habillé de noir et de chair rouge.

Or, ce septième homme
est un cheval,
un cheval avec un homme qui le mène.

TUTUGURI

THE RITE OF THE BLACK SUN

And below, as at the bottom of the bitter,
cruelly desperate slope of the heart,
the circle of the six crosses opens,
                    far below,
as if embedded in the mother earth,
disembedded from the filthy embrace of the mother
                    who slobbers.

The earth of black coal
is the only humid spot
in this cleft of rock.

The Rite is that the new sun passes through seven
        points before exploding at the earth's orifice.

And there are six men,
one for each sun,
and a seventh man
who is the sun completely
                    raw
dressed in black and red flesh.

Now, this seventh man
is a horse,
a horse with a man leading him.

Mais c'est le cheval
qui est le soleil
et non l'homme.

Sur le déchirement d'un tambour et d'une
    trompette longue,
étrange,
les six hommes
qui étaient couchés,
roulés à ras de terre,
jaillissent successivement comme des tournesols,
non pas soleils
mais sols tournants,
des lotus d'eau ;
et à chaque jaillissement
correspond le gong de plus en plus sombre
                et *rentré*
                du tambour
jusqu'à ce que tout à coup on voie arriver au grand
    galop, avec une vitesse de vertige,
le dernier soleil,
le premier homme,
le cheval noir avec un
                homme nu,
                absolument nu
                et *vierge*
                sur lui.

Ayant bondi, ils avancent suivant des méandres
    circulaires
et le cheval de viande saignante s'affole
et caracole sans arrêt
au faîte de son rocher
jusqu'à ce que les six hommes
aient achevé de cerner
complètement
les six croix.

But it is the horse
that is the sun
and not the man.

On the rending of a drum and of a long, peculiar
trumpet,
the six men
who were lying down,
rolled up flush with the ground,
spring up successively like sunflowers,
not suns at all
but turning soils,
lotuses of water,
and to each upspring
corresponds the increasingly gloomy
                    and *repressed*
                    gong
                    of the drum
until suddenly we see coming in full gallop, at
          vertiginious speed,
the last sun,
the first man,
the black horse with a
                    man naked,
                    absolutely naked
                    and *virgin*
                    on it.

Having gamboled, they advance following circular
     meanders
and the horse of bloody meat panics
and caracoles without stopping
on the top of its rock
until the six men
have finished encircling
completely
the six crosses.

Or, le ton majeur du Rite est justement
L'ABOLITION DE LA CROIX.

Ayant achevé de tourner
ils déplantent
les croix de terre
et l'homme nu
sur le cheval
arbore
un immense fer à cheval
qu'il a trempé dans une coupure de son sang.

Now, the major tone of the Rite is precisely
                    THE ABOLITION OF THE CROSS.

Having finished turning
they uproot
the earthen crosses
and the man naked
on the horse
raises high
an immense horseshoe
which he has tempered in a cut of his blood.

LA RECHERCHE DE LA FÉCALITÉ

Là où ça sent la merde
ça sent l'être.
L'homme aurait très bien pu ne pas chier,
ne pas ouvrir la poche anale,
mais il a choisi de chier
comme il aurait choisi de vivre
au lieu de consentir à vivre mort.

C'est que pour ne pas faire caca,
il lui aurait fallu consentir
à ne pas être,
mais il n'a pas pu se résoudre à perdre
            l'être,
c'est-à-dire à mourir vivant.

Il y a dans l'être
quelque chose de particulièrement tentant pour
        l'homme
et ce quelque chose est justement
            LE CACA.
            (*Ici rugissements.*)

Pour exister il suffit de se laisser aller à être,
mais pour vivre,
il faut être quelqu'un,
pour être quelqu'un,
il faut avoir un OS,

RESEARCH ON FECALITY

There where it smells of shit
it smells of being.
Man could very well have avoided shitting,
and kept his anal pocket closed,
but he chose to shit
like he could've chosen to live
instead of consenting to live dead.

The fact is that in order not to make caca,
he would've had to consent
not to be,
but he could not resolve to lose
                    being,
in other words to die alive.

There is in being
something particularly tempting for
    man
and that something is precisely
                    CACA
            (Roarings here.)

In order to exist you need only let yourself go to be,
but to live,
you must be somebody,
to be somebody,
you must have a BONE,

ne pas avoir peur de montrer l'os,
et de perdre la viande en passant.

L'homme a toujours mieux aimé la viande
que la terre des os.
C'est qu'il n'y avait que de la terre et du bois d'os,
et il lui a fallu gagner sa viande,
il n'y avait que du fer et du feu
et pas de merde,
et l'homme a eu peur de perdre la merde
ou plutôt il a *désiré* la merde
et, pour cela, sacrifié le sang.

Pour avoir de la merde,
c'est-à-dire de la viande,
là où il n'y avait que du sang
et de la ferraille d'ossements
et où il n'y avait pas à gagner d'être
mais où il n'y avait qu'à perdre la vie.

> **o reche modo**
> **to edire**
> **di za**
> **tau dari**
> **do padera coco**

Là, l'homme s'est retiré et il a fui.

Alors les bêtes l'ont mangé.

Ce ne fut pas un viol,
il s'est prêté à l'obscène repas.

Il y a trouvé du goût,
il a appris lui-même
à faire la bête
et à manger le rat
délicatement.

not be afraid of showing the bone,
and of losing the meat on the way.

Man has always preferred meat
to the earth of bones.
The fact is there was only earth and bone wood,
and he had to earn his meat,
there was only iron and fire
and no shit,
and man was afraid of losing shit
or rather he *desired* shit
and, for that, sacrificed blood.

In order to have shit,
in other words meat,
where there was only blood
and the scrap iron of bones
and where there was no question of earning being
but where there was one of losing life.

> **o reche modo**
> **to edire**
> **di za**
> **tau dari**
> **do padera coco**

There, man withdrew and fled.

Then the beasts ate him.

It was not a rape,
he lent himself to the obscene meal.

He found it tasty,
even he himself learned
to play the beast
and to eat rat
daintily.

Et d'où vient cette abjection de saleté ?

De ce que le monde n'est pas encore constitué,
ou de ce que l'homme n'a qu'une petite idée du
    monde
et qu'il veut éternellement la garder ?

Cela vient de ce que l'homme,
un beau jour,
a *arrêté*
                l'idée du monde.

Deux routes s'offraient à lui :
celle de l'infini dehors,
celle de l'infime dedans.

Et il a choisi l'infime dedans.
Là où il n'y a qu'à presser
le rat,
la langue,
l'anus
ou le gland.

Et dieu, dieu lui-même a pressé le mouvement.

Dieu est-il un être ?
S'il en est un c'est de la merde.
S'il n'en est pas un
il n'est pas.
Or il n'est pas,
mais comme le vide qui avance avec toutes ses formes
dont la représentation la plus parfaite
est la marche d'un groupe incalculable de morpions.

« Vous êtes fou, monsieur Artaud, et la messe ? »

Je renie le baptême et la messe.
Il n'y a pas d'acte humain

And where does this filthy abasement come from?

From the fact that the world is not yet formed,
or from the fact that man has only a faint idea of
the world
which he wants to keep forever?

That comes from the fact that man,
one fine day,
stopped
                    the idea of the world.

Two roads were offered to him:
that of the infinite outside,
that of the infinitesimal inside.

And he chose the infinitesimal inside.
Where it is only a question of squeezing
the rat,
the tongue,
the anus
or the glans.

And god, god himself hastened the movement.

Is god a being?
If he is it is made of shit.
If he is not
he's not.
Now, he is not,
but like the void which advances with all its forms
of which the most perfect representation
is the march of an incalculable group of crab lice.

"You are mad, Mr. Artaud, and the Mass?"

I abjure baptism and the Mass.
There is no human act

qui, sur le plan érotique interne,
soit plus pernicieux que la descente
du soi-disant Jésus-christ
sur les autels.

On ne me croira pas
et je vois d'ici les haussements d'épaules du public
mais le nommé christ n'est autre que celui
qui en face du morpion dieu
a consenti à vivre sans corps,
alors qu'une armée d'hommes
descendue d'une croix,
où dieu croyait l'avoir depuis longtemps clouée,
s'est révoltée,
et, bardée de fer,
de sang,
de feu, et d'ossements,
avance, invectivant l'Invisible
afin d'y finir le JUGEMENT DE DIEU.

which, on the internal erotic plane,
is more pernicious than the descent
of so-called Jesus christ
onto the altars.

No one will believe me
and from here I see the public shrugging its shoulders
but the named christ is no other than he
who facing the crab louse god
consented to live without a body,
while an army of men
descended from a cross,
where god believed he had long ago nailed them,
rebelled,
and, cased in iron,
in blood,
in fire, and bones,
advances, reviling the Invisible
in order to end GOD'S JUDGEMENT there.

LA QUESTION SE POSE DE...

Ce qui est grave
est que nous savons
qu'après l'ordre
de ce monde
il y en a un autre.

Quel est-il ?

Nous ne le savons pas.

Le nombre et l'ordre des suppositions possibles
    dans ce domaine
est justement
l'infini !

Et qu'est-ce que l'infini ?

Au juste nous ne le savons pas !

C'est un mot
dont nous nous servons
pour indiquer
l'ouverture
de notre conscience
vers la possibilité
démesurée,
inlassable et démesurée.

To Raise the Question of...

What is serious
is that we know
that after the order
of this world
there is another.

Which is it?

We do not know.

The number and order of possible suppositions
    in this domain
is precisely
infinity!

And what is infinity?

We do not exactly know!

It is a word
we employ
to indicate
the opening
of our consciousness
towards an immeasurable
possibility,
indefatigable and immeasurable.

Et qu'est-ce au juste que la conscience ?

Au juste nous ne le savons pas.

C'est le néant.

Un néant
dont nous nous servons
pour indiquer
quand nous ne savons pas quelque chose
de quel côté
nous ne le savons
et nous disons
alors
conscience,
du côté de la conscience,
mais il y a cent mille autres côtés.

Et alors ?

Il semble que la conscience
soit en nous
liée
au désir sexuel
et à la faim ;

mais elle pourrait
très bien
ne pas leur être
liée.

On dit,
on peut dire,
il y en a qui disent
que la conscience
est un appétit,
l'appétit de vivre ;

And what exactly is consciousness?

We do not exactly know.

It is nothingness.

A nothingness
we employ
to indicate
when we do not know something
from what side
we do not know it
and we say
then
consciousness,
from the side of consciousness,
but there are a hundred thousand other sides.

So what?

It seems that consciousness
is in us
linked
to sexual desire
and hunger;

but it could
very well
not be
linked to them.

It is said,
it can be said,
there are those who say
that consciousness
is an appetite,
the appetite for life;

et immédiatement
à côté de l'appétit de vivre,
c'est l'appétit de la nourriture
qui vient immédiatement à l'esprit ;

comme s'il n'y avait pas des gens qui mangent
sans aucune espèce d'appétit ;
et qui ont faim.

Car cela aussi
existe
d'avoir faim
sans appétit ;

et alors ?

Alors

l'espace de la possibilité
me fut un jour donné
comme un grand pet
que je ferai ;

mais ni l'espace,
ni la possibilité,
je ne savais au juste ce que c'était,

et je n'éprouvais pas le besoin d'y penser,

c'étaient des mots
inventés pour définir des choses
qui existaient
ou n'existaient pas
en face de
l'urgence pressante
d'un besoin :
celui de supprimer l'idée,
l'idée et son mythe,

and immediately
beside the appetite for life,
it is the appetite for food
which comes immediately to mind;

as though there were not people who eat
without any kind of appetite;
and who are hungry.

For that also
occurs
to be hungry
without appetite;

so what?

So

the space of possibility
was given me one day
like a loud fart
that I will let;

but neither the space,
nor the possibility,
I didn't know exactly what they were,

and I didn't feel the need to think about it,

they were words
invented to define things
which existed
or did not exist
confronted by
the pressing urgency
of a need:
that of abolishing the idea,
the idea and its myth,

et de faire régner à la place
la manifestation tonnante
de cette explosive nécessité :
dilater le corps de ma nuit interne,

du néant interne
de mon moi

qui est nuit,
néant,
irréflexion,

mais qui est explosive affirmation
qu'il y a
quelque chose
à quoi faire place :

mon corps.

Et vraiment
le réduire à ce gaz puant,
mon corps ?
Dire que j'ai un corps
parce que j'ai un gaz puant
qui se forme
au dedans de moi ?

Je ne sais pas
mais
je sais que

                        l'espace,
                        le temps,
                        la dimension,
                        le devenir,
                        le futur,
                        l'avenir,
                        l'être,
                        le non-être,

and of enthroning in its place
the thundering manifestation
of this explosive necessity:
to dilate the body of my internal night,

of the internal nothingness
of my self

which is night,
nothingness,
irreflection,

but which is an explosive assertion
that there is
something
to make way for:

my body.

And really
reduce my body to
this stinking gas?
To say that I have a body
because I have a stinking gas
which forms
inside me?

I don't know
but
I do know that
                space,
                time,
                dimension,
                becoming,
                the future,
                the hereafter,
                being,
                non-being,

le moi,
le pas moi,
ne sont rien pour moi ;

mais il y a une chose
qui est quelque chose,
une seule chose
qui soit quelque chose,
et que je sens
à ce que ça veut
SORTIR :
la présence
de ma douleur
de corps,

la présence
menaçante,
jamais lassante
de mon
corps ;

si fort qu'on me presse de questions
et que je nie toutes les questions,
il y a un point
où je me vois contraint
de dire non,

NON

alors
à la négation ;

et ce point
c'est quand on me presse,

quand on me pressure
et qu'on me trait
jusqu'au départ

the self,
the non-self,
are nothing to me;

but there is one thing
which is something,
only one thing
which is something,
and I feel it
because it wants to
COME OUT:
the presence
of my corporal
pain,

the menacing,
never tiring
presence
of my
body;

however much I am pressed with questions
and deny all questions,
there is a point
where I find myself forced
to say no,

NO

then
to negation;

and this point,
it's when I'm pressed,

when I'm squeezed out
and am milked
until the departure

en moi
de la nourriture,
de ma nourriture
et de son lait,

et qu'est-ce qui reste ?

Que je suis suffoqué ;

et je ne sais pas si c'est une action
mais en me pressant ainsi de questions
jusqu'à l'absence
et au néant
de la question
on m'a pressé
jusqu'à la suffocation
en moi
de l'idée de corps
et d'être un corps,

et c'est alors que j'ai senti l'obscène

et que j'ai pété
de déraison
et d'excès
et de la révolte
de ma suffocation.

C'est qu'on me pressait
jusqu'à mon corps
et jusqu'au corps

et c'est alors
que j'ai tout fait éclater
parce qu'à mon corps
on ne touche jamais.

within me
of food,
of my food
and its milk,

and what remains?

That I am suffocated;

and I don't know if it is an action
but by pressing me thus with questions
even to the absence
and the nothingness
of the question
I was pressed
even to the suffocation
within me
of the idea of body
and of being a body,

and it is then that I smelled the obscene

and that I farted
out of folly
and out of excess
and out of the revolt
of my suffocation.

The fact is I was being pressed
right up to my body
and right up to the body

**and it is then
that I shattered everything
because my body
is never to be touched.**

Conclusion

— Et à quoi vous a servi, monsieur Artaud, cette Radio-Diffusion ?.

— En principe à dénoncer un certain nombre de saletés sociales officiellement consacrées et reconnues :

1° cette émission du sperme infantile donné bénévolement par des enfants en vue d'une fécondation artificielle de fœtus encore à naître et qui verront le jour dans un siècle ou plus.

2° A dénoncer, chez ce même peuple américain qui occupe toute la surface de l'ancien continent indien, une résurrection de l'impérialisme guerrier de l'antique Amérique qui fit que le peuple indien d'avant Colomb fut abjecté par toute la précédente humanité.

3° — Vous énoncez là, monsieur Artaud, des choses bien bizarres.

4° — Oui, je dis une chose bizarre, c'est que les Indiens d'avant Colomb étaient, contrairement à tout ce qu'on a pu croire, un peuple étrangement civilisé

CONCLUSION

— And what has been your purpose, Mr. Artaud, in this radio broadcast?

— In principle to denounce a certain number of officially consecrated and acknowledged social filths:
1° this emission of infantile sperm given free of charge by children with a view to the artificial insemination of foetuses still to be born
that will see the light of day in a century or more.

2° To denounce, in this same American people who occupy the entire surface of the former Indian continent, a revival of the warlike imperialism of ancient America which caused the pre-Columbian Indians to be despised by all precedent mankind.

3° — You are expressing here, Mr. Artaud, some very bizarre things.

4° — Yes, I am saying something bizarre,
the fact is that the pre-Columbian Indians were, contrary to whatever one might have believed, a strangely civilized people

et qu'ils avaient justement connu une forme de civili-
sation basée sur le principe exclusif de la cruauté.

5°   — Et savez-vous ce que c'est au juste que la
      cruauté ?

6°   — Comme ça, non, je ne le sais pas.

7°   — La cruauté, c'est d'extirper par le sang
      et jusqu'au sang dieu, le hasard bestial de
      l'animalité inconsciente humaine, partout où on
      peut le rencontrer.

8°   — L'homme, quand on ne le tient pas, est un
      animal érotique,
il a en lui un tremblement inspiré,
une espèce de pulsation
productrice de bêtes sans nombre qui sont la forme
      que les anciens peuples terrestres attribuaient
      universellement à dieu.
Cela faisait ce qu'on appelle un esprit.
Or, cet esprit venu des Indiens d'Amérique ressort
      un peu partout aujourd'hui sous des allures
      scientifiques qui ne font qu'en accuser l'emprise
      infectieuse morbide, l'état accusé de vice, mais
      d'un vice qui pullule de maladies,
parce que, riez tant que vous voudrez,
mais ce qu'on a appelé les microbes
                  c'est dieu,
et savez-vous avec quoi les Américains et les Russes
      font leurs atomes ?
Ils les font avec les microbes de dieu.

— Vous délirez, monsieur Artaud.
Vous êtes fou.

— Je ne délire pas.
Je ne suis pas fou.

who had in fact known a form of civilization based
   on the exclusive principle of cruelty.

5° — And do you know exactly what cruelty is?

6° — Just like that, no, I don't know.

7° — Cruelty, it's to extirpate through the blood
   and as far as the blood god, the bestial risk of
   unconscious human animality, wherever it may
   be encountered.

8° — Man, when he is not held back, is an erotic
   animal,
he has within him an inspired tremor,
a sort of pulsation
producing innumerable beasts which are the form
   the ancient terrestrial peoples universally
   attributed to god.
That made what is called a spirit.
Now, this spirit which came from the American
   Indians is reappearing a little bit everywhere
   today in scientific guise which serves only to
   reveal this spirit's morbid infectuous hold, the
   salient state of vice, but a vice pullulating with
   diseases,
for, laugh as much as you wish,
what have been called microbes
                        is in fact god,
and do you know what the Americans and the
   Russians make their atoms with?
They make them with the microbes of god.

— You are raving, Mr. Artaud.
You are mad.

— I am not raving.
I'm not mad.

Je vous dis qu'on a réinventé les microbes afin
d'imposer une nouvelle idée de dieu.

On a trouvé un nouveau moyen de faire ressortir
dieu et de le prendre sur le fait de sa nocivité
microbienne.
C'est de le clouer au cœur,
là où les hommes l'aiment le mieux,
sous la forme de la sexualité maladive,
dans cette sinistre apparence de cruauté morbide
qu'il revêt aux heures où il lui plaît de tétaniser
et d'affoler comme présentement l'humanité.

Il utilise l'esprit de pureté d'une conscience
demeurée candide comme la mienne pour
l'asphyxier de toutes les fausses apparences qu'il
répand universellement dans les espaces et c'est
ainsi qu'Artaud le Mômo peut prendre figure
d'halluciné.

— Que voulez-vous dire, monsieur Artaud ?

— Je veux dire que j'ai trouvé le moyen d'en finir
une fois pour toutes avec ce singe
et que si personne ne croit plus en dieu tout le
monde croit de plus en plus dans l'homme.

Or c'est l'homme qu'il faut maintenant se décider à
émasculer.

— Comment cela ?
                Comment cela ?
De quelque côté qu'on vous prenne vous êtes fou,
mais fou à lier.

— En le faisant passer une fois de plus mais la
dernière sur la table d'autopsie pour lui refaire
son anatomie.

I'm telling you that microbes have been reinvented
in order to impose a new idea of god.

A new way has been found to make god come out
again and to catch him in the act of his
microbial noxiousness.
It's to nail him to the heart,
there where men love him best,
in the form of sickly sexuality,
in that sinister guise of morbid cruelty which he
dons in the hours when it pleases him as it does
now to tetanize and madden humanity.

He uses the spirit of purity of a consciousness that
has remained ingenuous like mine to asphyxiate
it with all the false appearances which he
spreads universally through the spaces and it
is thus that Artaud the Mômo can appear to be
hallucinating.

— What do you mean, Mr. Artaud?

— I mean that I have found the way to have done
once and for all with this monkey
and that if nobody believes anymore in god
everybody believes more and more in man.

And it is man that we must now decide to emasculate.

— How so?
How so?
From whatever angle one approaches you you are
mad, mad enough to tie down.

— By having him undergo once more but for the
last time an autopsy in order to remake his
anatomy.

Je dis, pour lui refaire son anatomie.
L'homme est malade parce qu'il est mal construit.
Il faut se décider à le mettre à nu pour lui gratter
        cet animalcule qui le démange mortellement,

                dieu,
                et avec dieu
                ses organes.

Car liez-moi si vous le voulez,
mais il n'y a rien de plus inutile qu'un organe.

Lorsque vous lui aurez fait un corps sans organes,
alors vous l'aurez délivré de tous ses automatismes
        et rendu à sa véritable liberté.

Alors vous lui réapprendrez à danser à l'envers
comme dans le délire des bals musette
et cet envers sera son véritable endroit.

I say, in order to remake his anatomy.
Man is sick because he is badly constructed.
We must decide to strip him in order to scratch out
    this animalcule which makes him itch to death,

            god,
            and with god
            his organs.

For tie me down if you want to,
but there is nothing more useless than an organ.

When you have given him a body without organs,
then you will have delivered him from all his
    automatisms and restored him to his true liberty.

Then you will teach him again to dance inside out
as in the delirium of dance halls
and that inside out will be his true side out.

LE THÉÂTRE
DE DA CRUAUTÉ

The Theater
of Cruelty

Connaissez-vous quelque chose de plus
    outrageusement fécal
que l'histoire de dieu
et de son être : SATAN,
la membrane du cœur
la truie ignominieuse
de l'illusoire universel
qui de ses tétines baveuses
ne nous a jamais dissimulé
que le Néant ?

En face de cette idée d'un univers préétabli,
l'homme n'est jusqu'ici jamais parvenu à établir
    sa supériorité sur les empires de la possibilité.

Car s'il n'y a rien,
il n'y a rien,
que cette idée excrémentielle
d'un être qui aurait fait par exemple les bêtes.

Et d'où viennent les bêtes
dans ce cas ?
De ce que le monde des perceptions corporelles
n'est pas à son plan,
et pas au point,

de ce qu'il y a une vie psychique
et aucune vie organique vraie,

de ce que la simple idée d'une vie organique pure
peut se poser,

Do you know anything more outrageously
      fecal
than the story of god
and of his being: SATAN,
the membrane of the heart
the ignominious sow
of the illusory universal
who with her slobbering udders
has never concealed anything from us
except Nothingness?

Facing this idea of a pre-established universe,
man has never succeeded up to now in establishing
      his superiority over the empires of possibility.

For if there is nothing,
there is nothing,
except this excremental idea
of a being who created for example the beasts.

And where do the beasts come from
in that case?
From the fact that the world of corporal perceptions
is not on its plane,
and not to the point,

from the fact that there is a psychic life
and no true organic life,

from the fact that the simple idea of a pure organic
life can be raised,

de ce qu'une distinction
a pu s'établir entre
la vie organique embryonnaire pure
et la vie passionnelle
et concrète intégrale du corps humain.

Le corps humain est une pile électrique
chez qui on a châtré et refoulé les décharges,

dont on a orienté vers la vie sexuelle
les capacités et les accents
alors qu'il est fait
justement pour absorber
par ses déplacements voltaïques
toutes les disponibilités errantes
de l'infini du vide,
des trous de vide
de plus en plus incommensurables
d'une possibilité organique jamais comblée.

Le corps humain a besoin de manger,
mais qui a jamais essayé autrement que sur le plan
    de la vie sexuelle les capacités incommensura-
    bles des appétits ?

Faites danser enfin l'anatomie humaine,

de haut en bas et de bas en haut,
d'arrière en avant et
d'avant en arrière,
mais beaucoup plus d'arrière en arrière,
d'ailleurs, que d'arrière en avant,

et le problème de la raréfaction
des denrées alimentaires
n'aura plus à se résoudre,
parce qu'il n'aura plus lieu,

from the fact that a distinction
could arise between
embryonically pure organic life
and the impassioned and concretely
integral life of the human body.

The human life is an electric battery
whose discharges have been repelled and castrated,

whose abilities and emphases
have been oriented toward sexual life
while it is made
precisely for absorbing
by its voltaic displacements
all the errant availabilities
of the infinity of the void,
of the increasingly incommensurable
holes of void
of a never fulfilled organic possibility.

The human body needs to eat,
but who has ever tested other than on the plane
of sexual life the incommensurable abilities
of the appetites?

Make human anatomy dance at last,

from top to bottom and from bottom to top,
from backward to forward and
from forward to backward,
but much more from backward to backward,
moreover, than from backward to forward,

and the problem of the rarefaction
of foodstuffs
will no longer have to be solved,
because there will no longer be a reason,

même, de se poser.

On a fait manger le corps humain,
on l'a fait boire,
pour s'éviter
de le faire danser.

On lui a fait forniquer l'occulte
afin de se dispenser
de pressurer
et de supplicier la vie occulte.

Car il n'y a rien
comme la soi-disant vie occulte
qui ait besoin d'être supplicié.

C'est là que dieu et son être
ont pensé fuir l'homme dément,
là, sur ce plan de plus en plus absent de la vie occulte
où dieu a voulu faire croire à l'homme
que les choses pouvaient être vues et saisies en
      esprit,
alors qu'il n'y a rien d'existant et de réel,
que la vie physique extérieure,
et que tout ce qui la fuit et s'en détourne
n'est que les limbes du monde des démons.

Et dieu a voulu faire croire à l'homme en cette
      réalité du monde des démons.

Mais le monde des démons est absent.
Il ne rejoindra jamais l'évidence.
Le meilleur moyen de s'en guérir
et de le détruire
est d'achever de construire la réalité.
Car la réalité n'est pas achevée,
elle n'est pas encore construite.
De son achèvement dépendra

even, for raising it.

The human body has been made to eat,
has been made to drink,
in order to avoid
making it dance.

It has been made to fornicate the occult
in order to avoid
grinding down
and executing occult life.

For nothing
deserves to be executed
as much as so-called occult life.

It is there that god and his being
thought to flee from demented man,
there, on that increasingly absent plane of occult life
where god wanted to make man believe
that things could be seen and grasped in
      spirit,
even though there is nothing existent and real,
except external physical life,
and that all that flees from it and turns away from it
is only the limbo of the demons' world.

And god wanted to make man believe in that
      reality of the demons' world.

But the demons' world is absent.
It will never meet with evidence.
The best way to cure oneself of it
and to destroy it
is to complete the construction of reality.
For reality is not completed,
is not yet constructed.
On its completion will depend

dans le monde de la vie éternelle
le retour d'une éternelle santé.

Le théâtre de la cruauté
n'est pas le symbole d'un vide absent,
d'une épouvantable incapacité de se réaliser dans
    sa vie d'homme.
Il est l'affirmation
d'une terrible
et d'ailleurs inéluctable nécessité.

Sur les pentes jamais visitées
du Caucase,
des Karpathes,
de l'Himalaya,
des Apennins,
ont lieu tous les jours,
nuit et jour,
depuis des années et des années,
d'épouvantables rites corporels
où la vie noire,
la vie jamais contrôlée et noire
se donne d'épouvantables et repoussants repas.

Là, les membres et organes réputés comme abjects
parce que
perpétuellement abjectés,
refoulés
hors des rapacités de la vie lyrique extérieure,
sont utilisés dans tout le délire d'un érotisme
    qui n'a pas de frein,
au milieu du déversement,
de plus en plus fascinant
et vierge,
d'une liqueur
dont la nature n'a jamais pu être classée,
parce qu'elle est de plus en plus incréée et
    désintéressée.

in the world of eternal life
the return of eternal health.

The theater of cruelty
is not the symbol of an absent void,
of an appalling incapacity for realizing itself in
    human life.
It is the affirmation
of a terrible
and moreover inescapable necessity.

On the never-visited slopes
of the Caucasus,
of the Carpathians,
of the Himalayas,
of the Apennines,
have been conducted everyday,
night and day,
for years and years,
appalling corporal rites
where the black life,
the never restrained and black life
gives itself appalling and repellent meals.

There, the limbs and organs considered vile
because
perpetually vilified,
driven back
outside the rapacities of exterior lyrical life,
are used in all the delirium of
    unbridled eroticism,
in the midst of the discharge,
increasingly fascinating
and virgin,
of a liquor
whose nature has always refused classification
because it is increasingly increate and
    impartial.

(Il ne s'agit pas spécialement du sexe ou de
    l'anus
qui sont d'ailleurs à trancher et à liquider,
mais du haut des cuisses,
des hanches,
des lombes,
du ventre total et sans sexe
et du nombril.)

Tout cela est pour l'instant sexuel et obscène
parce que cela n'a jamais pu être travaillé et
    cultivé
hors de l'obscène
et les corps qui dansent là
sont indétachables de l'obcène,
ils ont systématiquement épousé la vie obscène
mais il faut détruire
cette danse de corps obscènes
pour les remplacer par la danse
de nos corps.

J'ai été affolé
et tétanisé
pendant des années
par la danse d'un monde épouvantable de microbes
exclusivement sexualisés
où je reconnaissais
dans la vie de certains espaces refoulés
des hommes, des femmes,
des enfants de la vie moderne.

J'ai été tourmenté sans fin par les démangeaisons
    d'intolérables eczémas
où toutes les purulences de la vie érotique
    de la bière
se donnaient libre cours.

(It is not especially a question of the sex organ or
    the anus
which should moreoever be cut off and got
rid of,
but of the top of the thighs,
of the hips,
of the loins,
of the entire sexless belly
and of the navel.)

All this is for the moment sexual and obscene
because it has never been possible to work and to
    cultivate it outside the obscene
and the bodies that dance there
are undetachable from the obscene,
they have systematically embraced obscene life
but this dance of obscene bodies
must be destroyed
in order to replace them by the dance
of our bodies.

I have been crazed
and tetanized
for years
by the dance of an appalling world of exclusively
sexualized microbes
in which I recognized
in the life of certain repressed spaces
men, women,
children of modern life.

I have been endlessly tormented by the itchings of
    intolerable eczemas
in which all the purulences of the erotic life of the
    coffin
flowed at full vent.

Il n'est pas besoin de chercher ailleurs que dans ces
     danses rituelles noires
l'origine de tous les eczémas,
de tous les zonas,
de toutes les tuberculoses,
de toutes les épidémies,
de toutes les pestes
dont la médecine moderne,
de plus en plus déroutée,
se montre impuissante à trouver la cautérisation.

On a fait descendre à ma sensibilité,
depuis dix ans,
les marches des plus monstrueux sarcophages,
du monde encore inopéré des morts
et des vivants qui ont voulu
(et au point où nous en sommes, c'est par vice),
qui ont voulu vivre morts.

Mais je me serai tout simplement évité d'être malade
et avec moi
tout un monde qui est tout ce que je connais.

> o pedana
> na komev
>
> tau dedana
> tau komev
>
> na dedanu
> na komev
> tau komev
> na come
>
> copsi tra
> ka figa aronda

There is no need to seek anywhere except in these
     black ritual dances
the origin of all the eczemas,
all the shingles,
all the tuberculoses,
all the epidemics,
all the plagues
whose cauterization
modern medicine,
increasingly baffled, proves quite unable to achieve.

My sensibility has been forced to descend,
for ten years,
the steps of the most monstrous sarcophagi,
of the yet unoperated world of the dead
and of the living who have chosen
(and at the point where we are, it's through vice),
who have chosen to live dead.

But I will quite simply have avoided being sick
and with me
a whole world which is everything that I know.

> o pedana
> na komev
>
> tau dedana
> tau komev
>
> na dedanu
> na komev
> tau komev
> na come
>
> copsi tra
> ka figa aronda

ka lakeou
to cobbra

cobra ja
ja futsa mata

DU serpent n'y en
A NA

Parce que vous avez laissé aux organismes sortir
    la langue
il fallait couper aux organismes
leur langue
à la sortie des tunnels du corps.

Il n'y a la peste,
le choléra,
la variole noire
que parce que la danse
et par conséquent le théâtre
n'ont pas encore commencé à exister.

Quel est le médecin des corps rationnés de l'actuelle
    misère qui ait cherché à voir un choléra
    de près ?

En écoutant la respiration ou le pouls d'un malade,
en prêtant l'oreille, devant les camps de concentra-
    tion de ces corps rationnés de la misère,
aux battements de pieds, de troncs et de sexes
du champ immense et refoulé
de certains terribles microbes
qui sont
d'autres corps humains.

Où sont-ils ?
Au niveau ou dans les profondeurs
de certaines tombes

**ka lakeou
to cobbra**

**cobra ja
ja futsa mata**

**OF THE serpent isn't any of
IT NA**

Because you have allowed the organisms to put out
    their tongues
the organisms should have been
cut off
at the exit of the body's tunnels.

There is plague,
cholera,
black smallpox
only because the dance
and consequently the theater
have not yet begun to exist.

What doctor of the rationed bodies of present
    misery has ever sought to really examine
    a cholera?

By listening to the breathing or the pulse of a patient,
by lending an ear, facing the concentration camps
    of these rationed bodies of misery,
to the beating of feet, of trunks and sex organs
of the immense and repressed field
of certain terrible microbes
which are
other human bodies.

Where are they?
At ground level or in the depths
of certain tombs

en des endroits historiquement
sinon géographiquement insoupçonnés.

ko embach
tu ur ja bella
ur ja bella

kou embach

Là, les vivants s'y donnent rendez-vous
avec les morts
et certains tableaux de danses macabres
n'ont pas d'autre origine.

Ce sont ces soulèvements
où la rencontre de deux mondes inouïs se peint
　　　sans cesse
qui ont fait la peinture du Moyen Age,
comme d'ailleurs toute peinture,
toute histoire
et je dirai
toute géographie.

La terre se peint et se décrit
sous l'action d'une terrible danse
à qui on n'a pas encore fait donner
épidémiquement tous ses fruits.

in historically if not geographically
unsuspected places.

> **ko embach**
> **tu ur ja bella**
> **ur ja bella**
>
> **kou embach**

There, the living make appointments
with the dead
and certain paintings of *danses macabres*
have no other origin.

It is to these upheavals
where the meeting of two extraordinary worlds is
    unceasingly depicted
that we owe the paintings of the Middle Ages,
as moreover all paintings,
all history
and I will even say
all geography.

The earth is depicted and described
under the action of a terrible dance
to which all its fruits have not yet been
epidemically bestowed.

POST-SCRIPTUM

Là où il y a de la métaphysique,
de la mystique,
de la dialectique irréductible,
j'écoute se tordre
le grand côlon
de ma faim
et sous les impulsions de sa vie sombre
je dicte à mes mains
                    leur danse,
                    à mes pieds
                    ou à mes bras.

Le théâtre et la danse du chant,
sont le théâtre des révoltes furieuses
de la misère du corps humain
devant les problèmes qu'il ne pénètre pas
ou dont le caractère passif,
                    spécieux,
                    ergotique,
                    impénétrable,
                    inévident
                    l'excède.

Alors il danse
par blocs de
KHA, KHA

POST-SCRIPTUM

There where there is metaphysics,
mysticism,
irreducible dialectics,
I hear the huge
colon of my
hunger writhe
and under the impulses of its somber life
I dictate to my hands
              their dance,
              to my feet
              or to my arms.

The theater and the dance of song
are the theater of the furious rebellions
of the misery of the human body
facing the problems it does not penetrate
or whose passive,
              specious,
              quibbling,
              inscrutable,
              inevident nature
              excedes it.

So it dances
in blocks of
KHA, KHA

infiniment plus arides
mais organiques ;

il met au pas
la muraille noire
des déplacements de l'interne liqueur ;

le monde des larves invertébrées
d'où se détache la nuit sans fin
des insectes inutiles :
     poux,
     puces,
     punaises,
     moustiques,
     araignées,
ne se produit
que parce que le corps de tous les jours
a perdu sous la faim
sa cohésion première
et il perd par bouffées,
          par montagnes,
          par bandes,
          par théories sans fin
les fumées noires et amères
des colères
de son énergie.

infinitely more arid
but organic;

it brings to heel
the black rampart
of the internal liquor's displacements;

the world of invertebrate larvae
which from the endless night
of useless insects breaks away:
        lice,
        fleas,
        bedbugs,
        mosquitos,
        spiders,
occurs only
because the everyday body
has lost under hunger
its primal cohesion
and it loses in gusts,
        in mountains,
        in gangs,
        in endless theories
the black and bitter fumes
of its energy's
rage.

POST-SCRIPTUM

Qui suis-je ?
D'où je viens ?
je suis Antonin Artaud
et que je le dise
comme je sais le dire
immédiatement
vous verrez mon corps actuel
voler en éclats
et se ramasser
sous dix mille aspects
notoires
un corps neuf
où vous ne pourrez
plus jamais
m'oublier.

Post-Scriptum

Who am I?
Where do I come from?
I am Antonin Artaud
and if I say it
as I know how to say it
immediately
you will see my present body
fly into pieces
and under ten thousand
notorious aspects
a new body
will be assembled
in which you will never again
be able
to forget me.

LETTERS ON

TO HAVE DONE
WITH THE JUDGEMENT OF GOD

TO FERNARD POUEY

Ivry, 11 December 1947

Dear Sir,

When we were discussing my 'experiment'
              at making a broadcast
              for the Radio,
and the question came up of my fee as an *'actor'*,
I said to you:
I'll leave it to you,
appalled to have to get into such miserable discus-
sions of figures, and demands for more or less, when
the question that mattered for me was the work of
breaking through into a new direction,
I simply assumed that, on your side of things, you
would want to do the maximum
and it didn't occur to me that you would have
allowed me to be paid less even than any of my own
performers.
Although I can try to be *'indifferent'*,
it's necessary to eat,
be clothed,
take means of transport,
and that's why the figure of 3,190 francs allocated
to me *has suffocated me!*
That aside,
let me come back to the work that has been accomplished.
I believe you can find in it the best and the worst.
I had a considerable involvement in Radio before
the war

with Paul Deharme
at Radio-Information
and so the work I've done with you in no way rep-
resents an initial contact with this means of expression
but it's *vital*,
furthermore,
that the Director
Mr Guignard
the editors
and in general
all of those
with whom I've been dealing
understand
WHAT my intentions and wishes were.
If you approached the thing as a whole, you could
have the impression of a chaotic and intermittent
work
of a kind of risky and epileptic
cutting into pieces,
where the listeners' senses in limbo also have to
take
at random
whatever suits them.
------------- NO!!, that's not the case.
To have done with the judgement of our acts
    through destiny
    and by a force that is
    determining
    means articulating
    the intention at stake
    in a way
    that is totally new
in order to indicate that the rhythmic order of
things and that destiny itself have changed their
course,
there are, in the broadcast that I've made,

           enough elements that are
           grating,
           stabbing,
           out of kilter,
           detonating
that, once *edited* in a new order, they will give the
proof that the sought-for aim has been attained,
my duty has been to bring to you those elements.
Have I brought them to you?
Some of those elements are bad,
some of them, I believe, are excellent,
I am hoping you are going to be able to find that
attuned editor
who will know how to give, to those elements that
I've brought to you, the unforeseen values which I
wished them to hold.
With regards,

                            Antonin Artaud.

TO JEAN PAULHAN

Ivry-sur-Seine, 10 February 1948

Very dear friend,

1 copy,
of *Artaud the mômo*
signed and dedicated by my own hand,
and
1 copy
of
HERE LIES preceded by
THE INDIAN CULTURE
were sent to you at least 15 days if not 3 weeks ago,
if you haven't received them, it's because the office
receptionist at the N.R.F. has got hold of them and
you now have to do everything to demand them
back at all costs
because I did what was needed from my side
and
signed those copies with my own hand
specifically for you.
They must have been cast aside in some office or
other.
Those copies which I arranged to be sent to you are
on SPECIAL PAPER
but – I'm telling you this again – all of that hap-
pened nearly three weeks ago
so there must be someone who has got their hands
on them before they reached you, and you have to
get searching now and demand them back
because very clearly
– and it's not in the *spirit* of persecution to believe

this –
right now a cabal has been mounted against me and
which could have all kinds of repercussions.
This story of the Radio Broadcast is lamentable.
The texts may well appear in 'Combat' or as
a booklet
but you won't hear the sounds,
the sonorous xylophone passages,
the screams, the guttural noises and the voice,
all of which would have finally constituted a 1st
version of the Theatre of Cruelty.
It's a DISASTER for me.
Yours very sincerely.

Antonin Artaud.

TO FERNAND POUEY AND
RENÉ GUIGNARD

17 February 1948

Very dear friends,

I believe that what overwhelmed and impassioned certain people such as Georges Braque in hearing the Radio Broadcast 'The judgement of god' is, above all, the part with the sound effects and xylophonic passages, along with the poem read by Roger Blin and the one read by Paule Thévenin. It's vital to avoid spoiling the effect of those xylophonic passages through the prevaricating, dialectic and long-winded text at the beginning. I sent you an express mail to indicate a number of cuts for you to make and which would leave only a few sentences at the beginning and the end of the *'Introduction'*.
　　I urge you to make those cuts,
　　I urge you
　　– both of you –
　　to VERIFY that those cuts are strictly made.
　　Nothing must subsist in this Radio Broadcast which is liable to disappoint,
　　to cause boredom,
　　or to exasperate
　　an avid public that has been seized by all of the innovation which the sound effects and xylophonic passages bring about,
　　and which not even the Balinese, Chinese, Japanese and
Sinhalese theatres contain.

I'm therefore counting on both of you
to go ahead and make those cuts, because
they have not been made and I shake your hands in
friendship.

Antonin Artaud.

Open Letter to the

Reverend Father Laval

Sir,

All that is fine and that you recognize my right to
    totally and integrally express my *individuality*.
However singular it may be
and
heterogeneous it may appear.
But there is one thing you do not say
and which constitutes a fundamental reservation
    about this right of expression,
it is that you yourself were
and are
Bound by 2
        CAPITAL rites,
that is, when you uttered those words,
you were in reality
Bound by 2 rites
with your own consent
paralyzing
your hands.
The fact is that like every priest
you were
and are *bound*
by the 2 rites
of the *consecration*
and *elevation*
of the Mass.
The fact is that like every Catholic priest

you had said your Mass that very morning.
And the celebration of the ceremony
called Mass
includes in the foreground
those 2 rites of *binding*
which for me
are tantamount to a downright spell
Consecration
and
elevation
are
spells
      of a special
      but
      MAJOR order
which, if I may say so, capitalizes
         life,
which drains all the spiritual forces in such a
    direction that all that is body is reduced to
    nothingness
and nothing else remains except a certain
        psychic life
completely freed
but so free
that all the phantasms
of the spirit,
of pure spirit
can be given free rein there
and there occurs
the sinister and torrential expansion of the diluvian
    and antediluvian life
of obsessional beasts
and it is precisely against all this
      that we are struggling
because flagitious sexual life is behind the free
    expansions of the spirit
and that
is what

the consecration
and
elevation
of the Mass
have
without saying it
FREED.
There is a nauseating flocculation of the infectious
life of being
which the PURE BODY
repulses
but which
the PURE SPIRIT
accepts
and which the Mass
through its rites brings about.
And it is this flocculation
which maintains the present
life of this world
in the spiritual lower depths
into which it is forever plunging.
But this is what popular consciousness will never
understand
that a macerated and trampled body,
crushed and compiled
by the suffering and pains of being nailed to the cross
like the ever living body of Golgotha
will be superior to a spirit handed over to all the
phantasms of the interior life
which is merely the leaven
and the seed
for all the stinking phantasmagorical bestializations.

To Paule Thévenin

Tuesday 24 February 1948.

Paule, I'm very sad and disheartened,
my body is hurting me, everywhere,
but above all I have the impression that people were disappointed
by my radio broadcast.
Wherever *the machine* is
there's always the abyss and the void,
there exists a technical interference which deforms
and annihilates whatever you have created.
The poor opinions of M. and of A. are unjustified
but they must have had their point of departure in
that transition's weakening of my work,
that's why I'm never again going to get involved
with Radio,
and from now onwards will devote myself exclusively
to theatre
that is, in the way I conceive it,
a theatre of blood,
a theatre at which, at every performance,
corporeally
something is gained
not just for the performer but also for whoever
comes to see the performance,
moreover,
you are not performing,
it's an action.
In reality the theatre is the *genesis* of creation.
That is going to happen.
I had a vision this afternoon – I saw all those who

are going to follow me and who still do not totally have their bodies because pigs like those at the restaurant last night are eating too much. There are those who eat too much and there are others who, like me, cannot eat any longer without *spitting*.
Yours,

Antonin Artaud

Clayton Eshleman translated the fourth letter;
Stephen Barber translated the remainder of the letters.

ALIÉNATION
ET MAGIE NOIRE

ALIENATION AND
BLACK MAGIC

Les asiles d'aliénés sont des réceptacles
        de magie noire conscients et prémédités,

et ce n'est pas seulement que les médecins
        favorisent la magie par leurs thérapeutiques
        intempestives et hybrides,
c'est qu'ils en font.

S'il n'y avait pas eu de médecins
il n'y aurait jamais eu de malades,
pas de squelettes de morts
malades à charcuter et dépiauter,
car c'est par les médecins et non par les malades
        que la société a commencé.

Ceux qui vivent, vivent des morts.
Et il faut aussi que la mort vive ;
et il n'y a rien comme un asile d'aliénés pour
        couver doucement la mort, et tenir en
        couveuse des morts.

Cela a commencé 4000 ans avant Jésus-christ
cette thérapeutique de la mort lente,
et la médecine moderne, complice en cela
        de la plus sinistre et crapuleuse magie,
        passe ses morts à l'électro-choc ou à
        l'insulino-thérapie afin de bien chaque jour
        vider ses haras d'hommes de leur moi,
et de les présenter ainsi vides,
ainsi fantastiquement
disponibles et vides,

Insane asylums are conscious and premeditated
    receptacles of black magic,

and it is not only that doctors encourage magic
    with their inopportune and hybrid
    therapies,
it is how they use it.

If there had been no doctors
there would never have been patients,
no skeletons of the diseased
dead to butcher and flay,
for it is through doctors and not through
    patients that society began.

Those who live, live off the dead.
And it is likewise necessary that death live;
and there is nothing like an insane asylum for
    gently incubating death, and for keeping the
    dead in incubators.

It began 4000 years before Jesus christ
this therapy of slow death,
and modern medicine, an accomplice in this of
    the most sinister and crapulous magic,
    subjects its dead to electroshock or to insulin
    therapy so as daily to throughly empty its
    stud farms of men of their egos,
and to expose them thus empty,
thus fantastically
available and empty,

aux obscènes sollicitations anatomiques et
  atomiques
de l'état appelé **Bardo**, livraison du **barda**
  de vivre aux exigences du non-moi.

Le Bardo est l'affre de mort dans lequel
  le moi tombe en flaque,
et il y a dans l'électro-choc un état flaque
par lequel passe tout traumatisé,
et qui lui donne, non plus à cet instant
  de connaître, mais d'affreusement et
  déséspérement méconnaître ce qu'il fut,
  quand il était soi, quoi, loi, moi, roi, toi,
  zut et ÇA.

J'y suis passé et ne l'oublierai pas.

La magie de l'électro-choc draine un râle,
  elle plonge le commotionné dans ce râle
  par lequel on quitte la vie.

Or, les électro-chocs du Bardo ne furent jamais
  une expérience, et râler dans l'électro-choc du
  Bardo, comme dans le Bardo de l'électro-choc,
  c'est déchiqueter une expérience sucée par
  les larves du non-moi, et que l'homme
  ne retrouvera pas.

Au milieu de cette palpitation et de cette
  respiration de tous les autres qui assiègent celui
  qui, comme disent les Mexicains, raclant pour
  l'entamer l'ecorce de sa râpe,
  coule de tous côtés sans loi.

La médecine soudoyée ment chaque fois qu'elle
  présente un malade guéri par les
  introspections électriques de sa méthode,

to the obscene anatomical and atomic
    solicitations
of the state called **Bardo**, delivery of the **full kit**
    for living to the demands of the non-ego.

Bardo is the death throes in which the ego falls
    in a puddle,
and there is in electroshock a puddle state
through which everyone traumatized passes,
and which causes him, no longer at this moment
    to know, but to dreadfully and desperately
    misjudge what he was, when he was
    himself, his own elf, his fief, wife, life,
    tripe, damnit and THAT.

I went through it and I won't forget it.

The magic of electroshock drains a death rattle,
    it plunges the shocked into that rattle with
    which we leave life.

But, the electroshocks of Bardo were never an
    experiment, and to death rattle in the
    electroshock of Bardo, as in the Bardo of
    electroshock, is to mangle an experiment
    sucked by the larvae of the non-ego, and
    that man will not recapture.

In the midst of this palpitation and this
respiration of all the others who
    besiege the one who, as the Mexicans say,
    scraping to broach the bark with his grater,
    flows lawlessly from all sides.

Bribed medicine lies each time that it presents
    a patient cured by the electrical
    introspections of its method, as for me,

je n'ai vu, moi, que des terrorisés de la méthode,
incapables de retrouver leur moi.

Qui a passé par l'électro-choc du Bardo, et le Bardo
de l'électro-choc, ne remonte plus jamais
de ses ténèbres, et la vie a baissé d'un cran.
J'y ai connu ces moléculations souffle après souffle
du râle des authentiques agonisants.

Ce que les Tarahumaras du Mexique appellent
le crachat de la râpe, l'escarbille du charbon
sans dents.

Perte d'un pan de l'euphorie première qu'on eut
un jour à se sentir vivant, déglutinant et
mastiquant.

C'est ainsi que l'électro-choc comme le Bardo crée
des larves, il fait de tous les états pulvérisés
du patient, de tous les faits de son passé des
larves inutilisables pour le présent et qui
ne cessent plus d'assiéger le present.

Or, je le répète, le Bardo c'est la mort, et **la mort
n'est qu'un état de magie noire qui
n'existait pas il n'y a pas si longtemps.**

I've seen only those who have been terrorized by
the method, incapable of recovering their egos.

Who has gone through the electroshock of Bardo,
and the Bardo of electroshock, never climbs
up again from its tenebrae, and life has
slipped a notch.
I've known there these moleculations breath upon
breath of the death rattle of authentically
agonizing people.

What the Tarahumaras of Mexico call the spittle
of the grater, the cinder of toothless coal.

Loss of a slap of the first euphoria that you had
one day feeling yourself alive, swallowing
and chewing.

It is thus that electroshock like Bardo creates larvae,
it turns all the patient's pulverized states, all
the facts of his past into larvae which are
unusable in the present yet which never
cease beseiging the present.

Now, I repeat, Bardo is death, and **death is only a
state of black magic which did not exist
not so long ago.**

Créer ainsi artificiellement la mort comme la
médecine actuelle l'entreprend c'est
favoriser un reflux du néant qui n'a jamais
profité à personne,
mais dont certains profiteurs prédestinés de
l'homme se repaissent depuis longtemps.

En fait, depuis un certain point du temps.

Lequel ?

Celui où il fallut choisir entre renoncer à être
homme ou devenir un aliéné évident.

Mais quelle garantie les aliénés évidents de ce
monde ont-ils d'être soignés par
d'authentiques vivants ?

To thus create death artificially as present-day
   medicine attempts to do is to encourage a
   reflux of the nothingness which has never
   been to anyone's benefit,
but off which certain predestined human profiteers
   have been eating their fill for a long time.

Actually, since a certain point in time.

Which one?

That point when it was necessary to choose between
   renouncing being a man and becoming an
   obvious madman.

But what guarantee do the obvious madmen of this
   world have of being nursed by the
   authentically living?

STEPHEN BARBER

CLAYTON ESHLEMAN'S TRANSLATIONS OF ARTAUD'S 1946-48 RADIO WORKS

Clayton Eshleman's translations of Antonin Artaud's work
– the finest yet undertaken, and those that best seize the
intensive furore and engulfing intricacy of that work –
focus solely on Artaud's final period, from the last months
of his three-year incarceration at the asylum of Rodez in
southern France, and from the subsequent twenty-two
months of his life back in Paris, after his release from that
asylum, and extending until his death. That final period –
from the early months of 1946 until the moment of Artaud's
death on 4 March 1948 – is undoubtedly the richest, most
productive phase of his work, and possesses a fury and
discipline far beyond that of his work with the Surrealist
movement in the 1920s and his Theatre of Cruelty project of the 1930s. It is the period when Artaud's preoccupations are at their most livid and confrontational, but also
the period when he finally seizes control of his language,
and wields a unique and astonishing corporeal poetry.
It is also the period in which, after a decade of planning
projects that were never realized, and a further decade of
stultified asylum incarceration, Artaud finally unleashes

his work in forms that its own volatile velocity serves to create: the texts for radio transmission that are translated in this volume, a series of major poetic works and a huge number of fragments, and seventy or so large-scale drawings. There is no time remaining for linguistic frailty or for aesthetic hesitation in Artaud's last work: everything is projected from his body, immediately, simultaneously, infinitely. Over several decades of exacting work, from the 1960s to the 1990s, Eshleman – a prominent poet in his own right – translated all of Artaud's essential writings of that last period, from his major poetic works such as *Artaud the Mômo* and *Watchfiends and Rack Screams*, to his censored radio texts, to his writings on his drawings, and to his final fragments, publishing those translations in now-unavailable collections and in issues of the poetry magazine which he edited in that era, *Sulfur*.

Artaud's final period is the culmination of his life's work, but in a very particular, non-linear and even aberrant sense. It forms the intensification and projection of obsessions which are present in the very first of his writings as a young poet, thirty years earlier – above all, the desire for a new kind of human anatomy, and the reconfiguration or expunging of the mental world – but which are no longer cast in pre-ordained forms (such as those of the film synopsis or of the theatre manifesto which he had adopted in his work of the 1920s and 1930s), and instead are instilled within a pulsing, immediate poetry that struggles with itself, constantly remaking itself as a livid self-autopsying process. Following the collapse of his Theatre of Cruelty project in 1935, Artaud had embarked on a series of gruelling journeys that ended with his arrest and asylum incarceration in 1937: firstly to Mexico, to the village of Norogachic in the Tarahumara mountains, with the aim to take peyote and investigate the potential for a new culture of fire and corporeal transmutation; and then to Inishmore, one of the remote Aran Islands off the western coast of Ireland, where he intended to witness a literally apocalyptic event from the vantage-point of the huge pre-Christian hill-forts of that barren, wild island. The final period of his work forms the culmination of those journeys' headlong excavation into the boundaries of the human body and its culture. Finally, Artaud's last period is the terminal-point for his decade of asylum incarceration, in the sense of forming the negation and repudiation of what he viewed as society's forcible eradication of his work's virulence, notably through the near-fatal starvation and beatings he had endured at the third asylum, Ville-Evrard, and the series of fifty-one electroshock treatments he had received at the last asylum, Rodez, from its director, Gaston Ferdière, and his assistant, Jacques Latrémolière; the denunciation of what he had faced in the asylums remains a presence that constantly inflects and imparts an extreme combativeness to Artaud's final work.

Artaud has a distinctive set of preoccupations at the end of his life, which form the axis of the poetry, letters and fragments of his final period. Above all, for Artaud, the human body has become nullified and redundant – and must now be violently transformed, so that almost all of its organs are jettisoned (it was Artaud's call for a 'corps sans organes', notably in his texts for the radio broadcast *To have done with the judgement of god* – translated in their entirety here by Eshleman – that inspired the seminal theoretical work of the French philosophers Gilles Deleuze and Félix Guattari). Artaud imagines, plans and attempts to undertake that corporeal reactivation through the medium of language. He relentlessly disassembles and probes the elements of his own damaged body and thereby generates an unprecedented poetry of human fragmentation. The natural world, too, has been contaminated and wastelanded, rendered synthetic and despoiled, for Artaud, and now needs to be imbued with a new ferocity and turbulence that allies it to his visions for the human body. All evidence of society, religion, sexuality and medicine is anathema to Artaud, and their erasure is an urgent demand of his final work; only his resuscitated body, and the world it engenders, will endure. Finally, Artaud's last period is profoundly preoccupied with death, as a state of black-magic bewitchment deployed by social power to maintain itself; although Artaud was only forty-nine years old at the moment of his release from Rodez, he anticipated his imminent death, or declared that it had already taken place. In newspaper interviews given at the end of February 1948, within a week of his death, Artaud imagined moments in human history when death had not existed, and insisted those moments could be revivified through the determination not to die, and through a creative regime of hammer-blows and knife-incisions exacted against society's henchmen and assassins. On the last night of his life, Artaud wrote in his final notebook that he had been: 'tipped over/into death,/there where I ceaselessly eat/cock,/anus/and caca/at all my meals,/all those of THE CROSS.' His very last notebook text details his terminal confrontations with maleficent agents of society: 'the same individual/returns, then, each/morning (it's another)/to accomplish his/revolting, criminal/ and murderous, sinister/task which is to/maintain/a state of bewitchment in/me/and to continue to/render me/an eternally/bewitched man/etc etc'.[1]

Artaud moved across creative media in the final period of his life with extraordinary agility and a sense of oblivion directed towards the expectation that a poet need work only in one form. In the 1920s and 1930s, his work in cinema and theatre had been done on a sustained basis, only interrupted and stalled by the incessant financial obstacles to the accomplishment of his planned films and spectacles. His final work is undertaken in a different way: Artaud welds together his poems, his drawings and his sound-recordings, at speed, often so that they work in confrontation with one another. His primary medium at that time was that of the notebook, in which he inscribed textual fragments (some of them expanded or dictated into the form of major poetic works, as with *Artaud the Mômo*), notations about his preoccupations and daily life, work-in-progress towards the texts and screams he was preparing to record for radio transmission, and innumerable, densely rendered drawings of corporeal mutation, weapons and torture-instruments; sometimes, his notebooks are pierced-through, from cover to cover, with a constellation of blows from violently wielded pencil-points, pen-nibs or knife-blades. The pages and covers are stained with the traces of many fluids. The alacrity and ferocity with which Artaud wrote down his texts frequently tears-through or shreds the pages' thin paper. The three notebooks which Artaud prepared for his one public performance (alongside two private art-gallery readings) of the final period of his life – at the Vieux-Colombier theatre in January 1947 – are multiply overlayered, text upon text, as though the preparations for that unique performance (at which, on the night, Artaud discarded his notebooks and delivered an improvisation) required the obliteration of language itself and the annulling of representation. Artaud had begun using the medium of the notebook at the beginning of 1945, while still interned at the Rodez asylum, and continued deploying notebooks until the end of his life, by which time he had amassed a total of 406 notebooks. He bought the cheapest schoolchildren's notebooks, made of shoddy, discoloured wartime and immediate post-war paper, and jammed them, several at a time, into his jacket-pocket, folded vertically, on his journeys around Paris.

Artaud's way of working, after his release from Rodez in May 1946, demanded a mobile medium, which his notebooks provided. He lived, throughout his final twenty-two months, on the periphery of Paris, in the grounds of a private convalescence home in the industrial port-suburb of Ivry-sur-Seine (historically one of the most left-wing Parisian suburbs, from which a large contingent of fighters had left for the Spanish Civil War, ten years earlier); it had been a condition of his release from Rodez that he remained in an institution, although the Ivry clinic, where James Joyce's daughter Lucia had also been a patient, was a dilapidated and shambolic environment which accorded

Artaud a high degree of freedom of movement. He would leave by metro-train for central Paris each morning (Paris's metro line extension to Ivry-sur-Seine was only opened at the beginning of the month he moved there), taking his notebooks-in-progress with him, and spent his days on the move, meeting friends (his closest companions of the period were the actor Roger Blin, and the writers Arthur Adamov and Marthe Robert, all of whom he had known before his incarceration, alongside new, younger friends such as Paule Thévenin and Colette Thomas), writing alone in the cafes of St Germain-des-Prés, especially the Flore, or making the journey up to Montmartre in search of laudanum, heroin and chloral hydrate. He worked incessantly throughout the course of each day, often stopping in the street and standing upright as he inscribed texts into his notebooks, or working on metro-trains and buses; he would then take the last metro of the evening back to Ivry-sur-Seine. A young tubercular poet, Jacques Prevel, accompanied Artaud on many of his urban trajectories, and noted every detail in his journal (published in 1974, and re-issued, expanded, in 1994, as *En compagnie d'Antonin Artaud*), providing an exhaustive record, often hour by hour, of Artaud's working process during much of his final period.

Several months after arriving at the convalescence home, Artaud had requested that its director allow him to distance himself from its other patients, by moving into a derelict, two-room pavilion on the edge of its extensive, wooded grounds. Photographs of the eighteenth-century pavilion show its location as being alongside the high boundary-wall of the grounds, close to the main avenue of Ivry-sur-Seine (in an area that, following the convalescence home's demolition, became a public park); the pavilion's main room had an immense fireplace. Alongside his notebook-writings and notebook-drawings undertaken on his journeys around Paris, and during visits to friends' apartments, Artaud also worked extensively in his pavilion, in the mornings and at night. He had always dictated the final versions of his books, whenever he could persuade his publishers to provide him with a secretary or assistant; in 1933, the final version of his account of the life of the Roman Emperor, Heliogabalus, had been entirely dictated from working-notes. He continued this approach in the final period of his life, in collaboration with Paule Thévenin, who became a close friend for Artaud, performed for his radio work, and would edit the twenty-six-volume edition of his *Œuvres complètes* for the publisher Gallimard after Artaud's death. In particular, many of the texts from the *Interjections* section of his most ambitious poetic work of that era, *Watchfiends and Rack Screams*, were dictated over a four-month period, around the end of 1946, for that book-project commissioned by the publisher Louis Broder, then passed on to another publisher, K (and not eventually published until 1978). Taking dictation from Artaud was a demanding process, since he expectorated his intricate texts, partly composed from invented glossolaliac elements of language, and cut by long silences, while lying in bed in the mornings, often drinking coffee and chewing his breakfast at the same time; several transcribers, including the young editor (and future filmmaker) Chris Marker, lasted only for short periods of time, before a brisk, undaunted secretary, Luciane Abiet, took over. In 1993, Luciane Abiet gave an interview for a documentary film on Artaud's final period, *La véritable histoire d'Artaud le Mômo* (directed by Gérard Mordillat and Jérôme Prieur) in which she described her morning visits to Artaud's pavilion for the dictation of the *Interjections* texts, and the difficulties and near-impossibilities she faced in mediating the volatile, scrambled oral-content from Artaud's mouth into a written transcription.

Most of Artaud's large-scale drawings were also undertaken at his Ivry-sur-Seine pavilion; the drawings are mostly portraits – astonishing facial excavations and anatomical reconfigurations – of friends and visitors to the pavilion. The poem *The Human Face*, on those large-scale drawings, was written for a pamphlet that accompanied the sole exhibition of Artaud's drawings during his life-time, at the Galerie Pierre in July 1947, while *Ten Years that Language Has Been Gone* and *50 Drawings to Assassinate Magic* focus instead on the smaller drawings, intersected with texts, that Artaud inscribed in his 406 notebooks.

In the final months of his life, from the late summer of 1947 onwards, Artaud was largely incapacitated by ill-ness, addiction and exhaustion, and his pavilion became the main arena for his work. Although he still made occa-sional journeys into central Paris, Artaud remained mostly fixed in his pavilion, writing ever-more skeletal, violent and corrosive notebook-fragments, and still immersed in his reconfiguration of the human anatomy and of death, over the final weeks of his life.

Eshleman's translations of Artaud's final period refo-cused and transformed the perception of Artaud's work for its English-language readership on their initial publi-cations, and still do so, even more acutely, in DIAPHANES' new editions. Eshleman's translations, for the first time, present Artaud in English in an authentic form, rendered both with great creativity and erudition, and with an intricate and ferocious corporeality that matches Artaud's own; Eshleman translated Artaud with a comprehensive scholarly knowledge of the entirety of his work and of its multiple forms – the result of many decades of sustained engagement. Strangely, for a figure of Artaud's vast stat-ure and influence, the English-language translations of his work over the past sixty or more years have never oth-erwise reached the affinitive and sensorial intensity that Eshleman achieves. From the first translation of Artaud in 1958, the Grove Press edition of *The Theatre and its Double* – and passing through Jack Hirschman's City Lights *Artaud Anthology* of 1965, the British publisher John Calder's volumes of 1968–74, Susan Sontag's edition of *Selected Writings* in 1976, and more recent publica-tions – Artaud has often been banalized, sent askew, or has simply suffered the process of mis-representation he most feared and attacked. Hirschman's edition – a massive seller in the late 1960s, and the previous volume with a particular focus on Artaud's late work – demonstrates the combination of idiosyncrasy, misplaced enthusiasm and sheer ill-informedness that has often plagued English-language translations of Artaud. On receiving Hirschman's manuscript (the work of numerous translators) in 1964, its publisher, Lawrence Ferlinghetti, who had commissioned the anthology, wrote to Hirschman: 'I don't really understand how you operate... I do not understand your criteria for the *order*, or sequence, of the contents as a whole. It's not chronological, is it? What is it?'[2]; Artaud's close collaborator Paule Thévenin complained in a letter to Ferlinghetti: 'The more deeply I look into the work Hirschman has done, the more furious I become... How on earth, to be frank about this, could you have put your trust in a person who doesn't speak a word of French and also doesn't understand a word of it?'[3]. Even so, prior to Eshleman's translations, it was Hirschman's anthology that had provoked and actively perplexed – sometimes propelling them towards the original French – its hundreds of thousands of readers, such as Patti Smith, over several decades.

Since 1987, Artaud's drawings and notebooks have been exhibited many times, at Paris's Centre Georges Pompidou, New York's Museum of Modern Art, Vienna's Museum of Modern Art, and London's Cabinet Gallery, also transforming and realigning the perception of his work. The notebooks' curator at the Bibliothèque Nationale de France, Guillaume Fau, has accomplished invaluable work in making them accessible and in envisioning their eventual digitisation. The series of events at Cabinet Gallery, Whitechapel Gallery and Visconti Studio in London in 2018 (marking the seventieth anniversary of Artaud's death and the end of decades of constrictive copyright controls and bitter feuds among Artaud's heirs) demonstrated the immense and interconnected span of Artaud's work – poetry, sound, film, art – for the first time. This DIAPHANES series embodies that same aim of projecting the infinite span and profound strata of Artaud's work, evident most tangibly in its last moments, and for English-language readers in Eshleman's superb translations.

In translating the texts of Artaud's foremost radio work, *To have done with the judgement of god*, Eshleman used the French publisher Gallimard's *Œuvres complètes* edition, volume XIII, edited anonymously by Paule Thévenin and published in 1974. The texts had previously been published as a book shortly after Artaud's death in 1948 by the publisher K éditeur, though the *Œuvres complètes* edition draws from the entirety of Artaud's manuscript notebooks used in the preparation for the project, alongside other documents. Eshleman also consulted the audio recordings of the work, including that issued by Sub Rosa Aural Documents, Brussels, edited by Marc Dachy.

Artaud's radio works extend from the very beginning of his time in Ivry-sur-Seine, after his release from the asylum of Rodez, until his death. Although *To have done with the judgement of god* is by far Artaud's best-known and most innovative radio work, he also recorded two of his texts for radio in June and July 1946: *The Patients and the Doctors*, on 8 June (it was transmitted on the following day) and *Alienation and Black Magic* on 16 July (again, it was transmitted on the following day). *Alienation and Black Magic* also appeared in Artaud's poetry collection *Artaud the Mômo*, translated by Eshleman from the *Œuvres complètes* volume XII; the text is also included in this volume in its status as simultaneously a poem *and* a radio work. (Artaud also sent the text to the newspaper *Combat* so that it would additionally form a public anti-psychiatric manifesto addressed to a mass audience, but it was not published there.) All of Artaud's radio works were commissioned by the French national radio station, which had been involved in commissioning and promoting experimental works and projects by artists and poets since the 1920s. Artaud was dissatisfied with his first two recordings, and only returned to the radio medium in the autumn of 1947, when he was invited to prepare a large-scale work. He recorded recently-written texts, and wrote several new texts for the project. The first recording session took place on 29 November 1947, with Artaud reading his work along with three collaborators: Paule Thévenin, Maria Casarès and Roger Blin. He returned to the recording studio on 16 January 1948 with Roger Blin to record screams, percussion, xylophone passages and other sound effects that were then incorporated into the previously recorded elements.

After his release from the Rodez asylum, Artaud was deeply concerned – more so than at any other point in his life – with the potential audience for his work. In part, he wanted to denounce, to the maximum number of people, his treatment at Rodez and the other asylums in which he had been incarcerated, as well as to transmit his preoccupations with anatomical reconfiguration and the annulling of all religious and societal forms. The two ways open to him were the medium of radio and via publications in France's national newspapers. Throughout the last period of his life, he wrote often to the editors of France's newspapers, demanding that his texts or letters should be included in them. In 1947, he wrote to Albert Camus, then editor-in-chief of the newspaper *Combat*: 'The erotic sexual life of France is sombre, Mr Albert Camus, it is as black as its black-markets...'.[4] Although his letter to Camus was not published in *Combat*, that newspaper in particular agreed to publish several of Artaud's writings. In an alliance of those two approaches to Artaud's audience, shortly after his death, one of the texts for *To have done with the judgement of god* was published in *Combat*. The opening text for that radio work is pitched in an urgent, contemporary tone, as though Artaud's report on the instigation of new armies for the emergent Cold War were a radio reportage.

Artaud's collaborators for *To have done with the judgement of god* were his close friends Paule Thévenin – a young medical student who had met Artaud when she was asked to be the intermediary in the commissioning of his first radio work in June 1946 – and Roger Blin – later a prominent theatre director of works by Genet and Beckett, but known in 1947–48 as a young actor and activist – along with Maria Casarès, an ascendant young Spanish actress who, as with Blin, would act in Jean Cocteau's film *Orphée* in 1950. Artaud had intended his friend Colette Thomas to read the text eventually read by Maria Casarès, but she declined to do so at the last moment, 'out of stubbornness', as Paule Thévenin told me, thereby necessitating a replacement.[5]

Artaud prepared the texts for *To have done with the judgement of god* in notebook versions during the weeks preceding the recording session on 29 November 1947. The text *The Theatre of Cruelty*, translated by Eshleman, was written especially for the radio project, and was fully prepared for inclusion, but had to be set aside on the day of the recording session since the other texts already recorded (along with the passages of sound effects still to be recorded at the session on 16 January 1948) completely filled the time available, so that it was not recorded. In his notebooks, Artaud also wrote about his radio work's aim to repudiate and annul the process of representation itself: 'There is nothing I abominate and execrate more than the idea of spectacle, of representation/that is, of virtuality, of non-reality,/attached to all that is produced and shown...'[6] Those fragmentary texts written immediately in advance of the recording session form an unprecedented exploratory amalgam of theory, dance manifesto, and sound-art experimentation, interrogating Artaud's irreligious preoccupations with anatomical reconfiguration, and projecting his contestations of power-driven subjugation and the fraudulent social status of madness.

To have done with the judgement of god was censored abruptly by the director of the French national radio station on the day before its planned transmission on 2 February 1948. It was censored for obscenity and blasphemy. The decision outraged many artists and writers as well as Artaud himself and his collaborators. Artaud was angry and disheartened; he wrote to his friend, the writer and

publisher Jean Paulhan, on 12 February 1948: 'LAMEN-
TABLE that the recording wasn't transmitted. You would
have finally seen what the *Theatre of Cruelty* could have
been.'[7] Many of his final letters are concerned with the
radio work's censorship and the attempts by his friends
to organise events at which the recording could be heard,
in the last-ditch hope that influential figures (such as
Jean Cocteau and Georges Braque) would attend and then
protest loudly enough that the censorship would be over-
turned. The last event took place in a cinema auditorium
in central Paris on 23 February, ten days before Artaud's
death. At the very end of February, the newspaper *Combat* sent a journalist to interview Artaud at his pavilion
in Ivry-sur-Seine, but by that point he had lost interest in
the furore over his radio work, and was preoccupied solely
with his imminent death, which took place in the night
of 3–4 March.

The censorship of *To have done with the judgement of
god* was not revoked. Over the following four decades, the
work almost vanished, subsisting only through the radio
station's archival copy and in obsolete reel-to-reel copies
preserved by the participants Paule Thévenin and Roger
Blin, who donated his copy to a theatre archive before
his death in 1984. From 1986, the recording began to re-
emerge, with its issuing as a vinyl record by La Manufac-
ture, then as the Sub Rosa CD heard by Eshleman and as
a set of CDs by the publisher André Dimanche in 1995
(including recordings of Artaud's two other radio works,
and a recording of what the French national radio station actually transmitted on 2 February 1948 instead of
Artaud's *To have done with the judgement of god*). Now the
recording is widely available online, for example on ubu.
com.

As they increasingly will do in the future, Artaud's
radio works of 1946–48 now form a source of deep inspiration for contemporary musicians, choreographers, artists, theorists, writers and poets. Eshleman's translations
of *To have done with the judgement of god* and *Alienation*

and Black Magic – along with the translations of letters by
Artaud on his radio works – aim to transmit that prolifer-
ating inspiration, text to voice, text to scream, text to art,
text to body, and onwards.

NOTES

1 Artaud, *Notebook 406*, 3–4 March 1948, unpublished, collection of the
Bibliothèque Nationale de France, Paris.

2 Ferlinghetti, *Letter of 17 February 1964*, unpublished, collection of the
Doheny Library, USC, Los Angeles.

3 Thévenin, *Letter of 20 November 1965*, unpublished, collection of the
Doheny Library, USC, Los Angeles.

4 Artaud, undated (1947) letter to Albert Camus, *La Nouvelle Revue Fran-
çaise*, issue 89 (May 1960), page 1017.

5 Interview with Paule Thévenin, Paris, 22 March 1987.

6 Artaud, notebook text, November 1947, *Œuvres complètes*, vol. XIII,
(Paris: Gallimard, 1974), page 258.

7 Artaud, *Letter of 14 February 1948*, unpublished, collection of the Bibliothèque Nationale de France, Paris.

Contents

© DIAPHANES 2021
ISBN 978-3-0358-0250-4

All rights reserved

DIAPHANES
Limmatstrasse. 270 | CH-8005 Zurich
Dresdener Str. 118 | D-10999 Berlin
57 Rue de la Roquette | F-75011 Paris

Printed in Germany
Layout: 2edit, Zurich

www.diaphanes.net